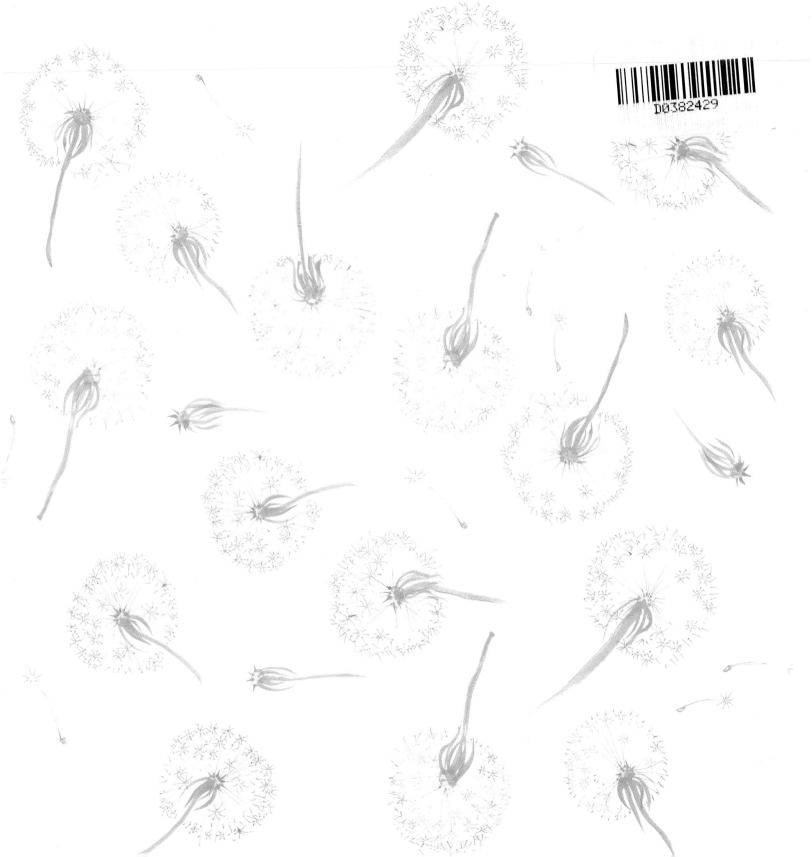

With love,
to Johnny
and our mama Betty,
who sang songs to us.

Suzy Spafford used 3B graphite pencil and transparent watercolor
on cold press illustration board to create the illustrations for this book.

Book design by Yolande Fejes

Published by Suzy's Zoo®
9401 Waples Street, Suite 150, San Diego, California, USA

Library of Congress Cataloging-in-Publication Data
Spafford, Suzy
Witzy and Zoom-Zoom/story and illustrations by Suzy Spafford.
Summary: Witzy Quacker doesn't want to take a nap and a fast moving
grasshopper lures the baby duck out of bed and into a backyard full of surprises!
[1. Baby duck-fiction 2. Childhood memories-fiction] I. Suzy Spafford, ill. II. Title
98-90889
ISBN 0-9643588-1-6
First edition 1998

Witzy and Zoom Zoom

by Suzy Spafford

It was naptime.
Witzy was nestled in
Mama's laundry basket
with all the favorite sleepytime toys.

But Witzy wasn't sleepy.
Not one tiny bit!

Witzy turned Lulla Bye's golden key to play them a tune.

Patches sat on the grass
and watched,
and Boof leaned back to listen.

As Lulla Bye's music
lifted in the breeze,
the sheets
flapped and fluttered
and the duck jammies did a little dance.

A blue butterfly soared overhead.
Boof was so excited,
he tumbled onto the grass.

And then,
JUST then...

something went
ZOOM ZOOM!

It sailed right over Witzy's top feathers.

What was that and
Where did it go?

"Zoom Zoom," said Witzy.
"Over there!"

As Patches, Lulla Bye,
and Boof watched
in wonder,
Witzy climbed out of the basket.

"I will find Zoom Zoom,"
Witzy squeaked
and toddled off into the grass.

A flutter of wings startled Witzy.
"You're not Zoom Zoom."

Witzy chased the butterfly...

until it fluttered up and up, high into the sky.

Witzy wandered into
a forest of tall grass.
"Oh! a tickle bug."

"Hee, hee!" giggled Witzy.
"Lots of tickles."

Witzy spied a funny bug moving
closer and closer.

"I see you. Peek-a-boo!"

Then something startled Witzy. Something that went ZOOM ZOOM!

"There goes zoom ZOOM!"

Witzy scampered after him,
but Zoom Zoom was too fast.

Patches watched,
Lulla Bye blinked,
and Boof didn't notice
anything until...

Zoom Zoom landed
right on top of his nose!
Then Boof went

Aaah... AaAH...AAAH...

CHOO!

And Zoom Zoom jumped up on the jammies.

The jammies gave a little kick,
and Zoom Zoom soared off
high into the sky...higher and higher.

"Bye-bye, Zoom Zoom!"
called Witzy.

Patches watched,
Lulla Bye waved,

and Boof gave a bear's sigh.

Up in the sky, ducks and elephants tumbled.

A bunny rabbit chased a butterfly.

Witzy made a
big, sleepy yawn.

And just in time...

Mama appeared.
As she gently carried Witzy,
she sang a whispery song:

"Witzy Witzy Woo,
Witzy Witzy Boo...
Zoom-ity zoom,
Bug-ity boom,
I love you.

Witzy Witzy Woo,
Witzy Witzy Boo...
Zoom-ity zoom,
Bug-ity boom,
I love you.

Witzy Witzy Woo,
Witzy Witzy Boo...
Zoom-ity zoom,
Bug-ity boom,
I love you."

Witzy and Boof
fell asleep as
Patches watched
and Lulla Bye played
a sleepy tune.

And Witzy dreamed
a backyard dream

of Zoom Zoom and
tickle bugs
and wonderful things.

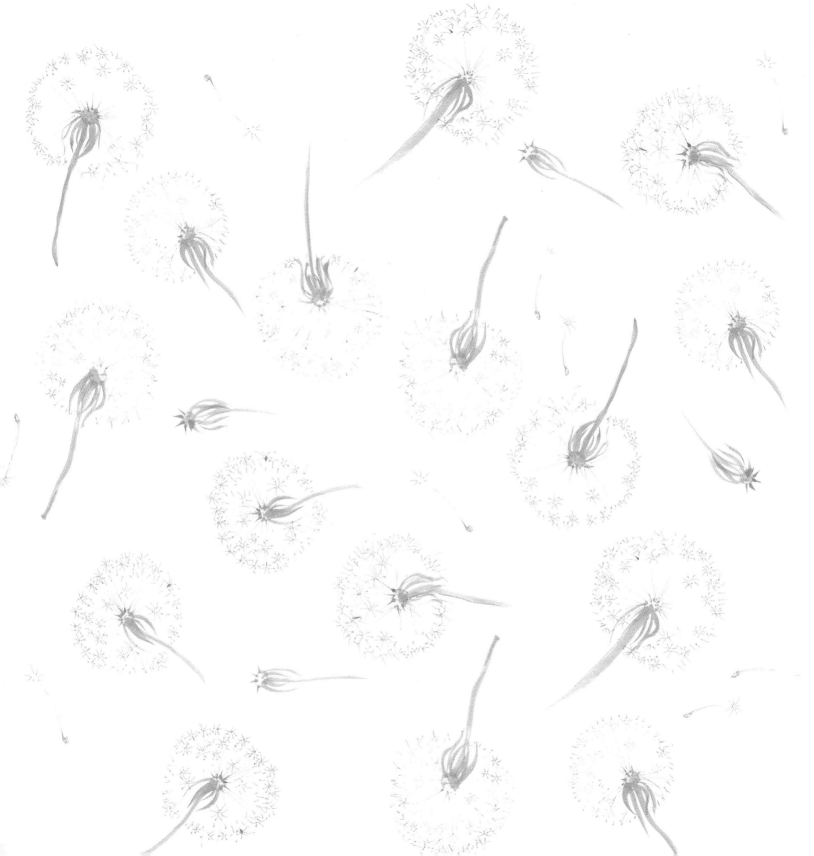